STONE Pizza

by **Susan K. Mitchell**

illustrated by **McNevin Hayes**

The RGU Group • Tempe, Arizona

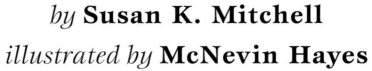

The illustrations were rendered in acrylic paint on board.
The text type was set in Esprit Book.
The display type was set in Chlorinar and BrushStroke.
Composed in the United States of America.
Graphic layout by Adriana Patricia De La Roche.
Production supervision by Laura Bofinger.

Printed in Singapore

First impression

Library of Congress Cataloging-in-Publication Data
Mitchell, Susan K.
  Stone pizza / by Susan K. Mitchell ; illustrated by McNevin Hayes.
      p. cm.
  Summary: Retells the classic tale with a southwestern setting and a clever
coyote who finds a way to get the other animals to share their food with him.
  ISBN-13: 978-1-891795-26-8 (hard cover)
  ISBN-10: 1-891795-26-0 (hard cover)
  [1. Folklore.] I. Hayes, McNevin, ill. II. Title.
  PZ8.1.M6936St 2007
  398.2--dc22
  [E]
                                                    2006028458

The RGU Group

www.theRGUgroup.com

10 9 8 7 6 5 4 3 2 1 (hc)

With love for Emily and Rachel, my own cool critters.
— *S.M.*

For Debra and for Nathan, eternally and infinitely.
— *McN, the Lucky*

Coyote's belly rumbled louder than a pickup truck as he wandered beside the highway. He hadn't eaten for days.

Summer brushfires and a long drought had made food scarce on this stretch of road and the local critters were especially suspicious of strangers. Everywhere Coyote walked, animals scurried into their burrows or scampered away.

Looks like hospitality is going to be as hard to find as food, thought Coyote. But luckily, Coyote was as clever as he was hungry.

So, he stopped to rest for a spell and come up with a plan. Then, he heard Horned Toad snoring loudly on a big, flat stone.

"Pssst! Pardon me, partner," Coyote said, waking up the sleeping lizard. "Do you know where a fella might find a bite to eat?"

"Hmmph! Sorry stranger," said Horned Toad. "Around here, food is harder to find than a flea on a June bug." Then, Horned Toad scurried into the scrub brush.

Looks like these folks need to learn how to make Stone Pizza, thought Coyote.

He picked up the stone Horned Toad had been sunning on and licked his chops as he gathered tumbleweeds to make a fire. Coyote placed the stone on top as he blew on the flames, and then he danced and sang.

"Stone Pizza … what a treat! I can hardly wait to eat!" Coyote said in his loudest voice. He made such a ruckus that critters began to peek out of their hiding places.

Horned Toad crawled out for a closer look. "What are you up to, mister?" he asked.

"Makin' Stone Pizza," Coyote replied. "The most lip-smackin' pizza you ever tasted."

"Looks like a plain old stone to me!" grumbled Horned Toad.

"Think so, do ya?" said Coyote. Horned Toad rolled his eyes and crawled back in the shade to watch. Soon, other critters came around for a closer look, too.

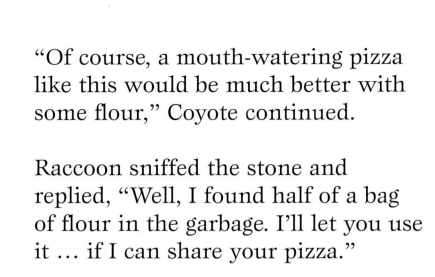

"Of course, a mouth-watering pizza like this would be much better with some flour," Coyote continued.

Raccoon sniffed the stone and replied, "Well, I found half of a bag of flour in the garbage. I'll let you use it … if I can share your pizza."

"Stale old flour from a trash can bandit!" mumbled Horned Toad.

"Deal!" said Coyote. Raccoon hurried off to fetch the flour.

When Raccoon returned, Coyote added water and kneaded it into dough. He flattened it out, gave it a toss in the air, and patted it down on the warm rock.

"Now if only I could round up some tomato sauce…" said Coyote, loud enough for all to hear.

Tortoise crept up to Coyote and said, "I saw a can a mile back by the picnic area. I don't know how you'll open it, but I'll get it … if I can share your pizza."

"Deal!" said Coyote. "Meet back here at sunset." Fortunately, there were no cars in sight as Tortoise ambled across the highway to fetch the sauce.

"You'll be lucky to get it by next Tuesday at his speed!" groaned Horned Toad.

Coyote ignored Horned Toad and continued fanning the flames. "I remember my ol' Grandpappy made Stone Pizza with cheese and mushrooms," he said. "Too bad we don't have any."

"I'd hate to give it up, but I've been saving a hunk of cheese for a special occasion," said Field Mouse.

"And I ran across some mushrooms while I was digging," offered Armadillo.

Horned Toad grumped, "Doesn't that sound delicious … moldy cheese and dirty mushrooms."

Coyote agreed to share with Armadillo and Field Mouse. A few minutes later, they returned with the cheese and mushrooms. The hungry critters watched Coyote break the ingredients into tiny pieces and toss them on top of the dough.

"Now, Grandpappy told me in some parts that Stone Pizza tastes even better with peppers and onions," said Coyote.

"Hey! There's a pepper garden a little ways from here," said Jack-rabbit.

"And I keep an onion in my burrow," said Skunk. "We'll let you use them … if we can share your pizza."

"Pilfered peppers and a smelly old onion from a skunk – phew!" said Horned Toad.

"Deal!" said Coyote. Jackrabbit bounded off into the brush as Skunk waddled off to her burrow. When they returned, Coyote set about dicing peppers and peeling the onion.

As the sunset burned bright orange and faded to pink, Coyote kept the fire going. Everyone gathered around with their mouths watering… everyone except Tortoise.

"I told you he'd never make it back in time!" said Horned Toad. "You couldn't open that can anyway."

Just then, Coyote saw Tortoise by the
side of the highway rolling a can with
his head. Coyote ran over to Tortoise
and picked up the can.

"Good timing, Tortoise!" said Coyote. "And now … for the big finish!" Off on the horizon, a huge 18-wheeler was speeding down the highway in a cloud of dust. Coyote carried the can to the edge of the road. The critters waved their paws and yelled at him to stop. Coyote gave the can a hard toss into the road.

"Great! Now we'll never get this pizza finished," said Horned Toad.

The truck got closer … and CLOSER … AND CLOSER … until …

SPLAT!!!

The animals opened their eyes and saw Coyote grinning by the side of the highway.

Coyote picked up the squashed can of sauce. "Yep, just enough left for our Stone Pizza."

Coyote added the sauce to the pizza. Just as the dough browned and the cheese and sauce bubbled, Horned Toad crawled out from the scrub brush.

"Can I help ya, partner?" Coyote asked.

Horned Toad lowered his eyes and cleared his throat. "Um, I er ... well ... I have something for the pizza, too ... if I can share." He pulled out two big crickets.

"Well, that's mighty nice, Toad ... but why don't you save those for YOUR slice," said Coyote.

When the pizza was ready, Coyote gave a slice to each critter — even Horned Toad. As they rubbed their bellies, all the critters thanked clever Coyote for showing them how to make Stone Pizza.

"Some dessert sure would be good," said Coyote.

"I bet we can use that stone to make Prickly Pear Pie," said Horned Toad. The other critters looked at each other and nodded.

Coyote smiled and said, "Toad, that just might work. Let's get cookin'!"